The Emperor's New Clothes

By *Hans Christian Andersen*

Adapted by *Rebecca Bondor*

Illustrated by *Richard Walz*

A GOLDEN BOOK • NEW YORK

Western Publishing Company, Inc., Racine, Wisconsin 53404

O nce there was an emperor who was very
vain. The only thing he cared about was his
wardrobe of beautiful clothes. All day long the
emperor tried on handsome new outfits and admired
his reflection in the royal mirror.

Weavers from his kingdom eagerly waited in line
to show their finest cloth to the emperor. They knew
he would pay them well for suits made from their
best fabrics.

Two tricksters from a neighboring kingdom heard about the vain emperor and hurried to the palace. The two had a plan. They would fool the emperor out of his gold and be rich for the rest of their lives.

At a meeting with the emperor, one trickster claimed, "We make the finest fabric in the land. In fact, our fabric is unbelievably wonderful. You could even say it is magical—since it can be seen only by the very wise."

The emperor was excited. Soon he would have the most wonderful clothes in the land *and* he would know which of his subjects were wise and which were fools. "I must have a suit of this extraordinary fabric made for me at once!" exclaimed the emperor.

He paid the two men in gold to begin their weaving.

The tricksters set up their looms in the royal weaving room. Then they pushed the shuttles hard for hours on end. The work made them sweat and frown. But they did not lace one bit of silk thread through the looms. The two only pretended to be making beautiful new fabric.

Meanwhile the emperor could think of nothing but the splendid new cloth. He was eager to visit the weaving room, yet he worried about the cloth's magical power. "What if I am not wise enough to see it?" he wondered.

The emperor decided to send his wisest minister instead. "Come back to me with a full report," the emperor instructed.

When the tricksters pretended to hold up the new cloth, the minister's heart skipped a beat. "Oh, my," he thought. "I see nothing at all!"

But the minister did not want the emperor to know he was not wise. "I will see to it that you get even more gold for the wonderful work you have done," said the minister. "And I will advise the emperor to come see the fabric for himself."

The emperor heard the minister's report and was
delighted. He went straight to the weaving room with
his most trusted courtiers.

Again the tricksters were pushing their shuttles
back and forth across the looms. When the courtiers
saw this, each one was taken by surprise. Not one of
them could see any cloth, for there was none to be seen.

"Aren't the colors and patterns beautiful?" asked the minister who had been there before.

"Indeed," remarked the courtiers. And they all nervously agreed that this fabric was most exquisite.

Now it was the emperor's turn to be worried. "I see no cloth at all. Not even a single thread," he thought to himself. "It seems that everyone else in my kingdom sees the material. Could it be that I am a simpleton, that I am unfit to be emperor?"

At that moment one of the tricksters suggested
the emperor come take a closer look.

"Your Highness, we have yet to hear if you like our
handiwork," he said.

The emperor knew better than to admit he saw
nothing. Instead he proclaimed he would wear a suit
made from the fantastic cloth in the next Royal
Procession.

"Begin the sewing at once!" he commanded.

That night, as many candles burned, the trickster snipped and sewed, pretending to make the new suit.

One trickster used his huge scissors to cut imaginary pieces of fabric in the emperor's size.

The other carefully sewed the invisible pieces
together. Of course, there was no thread in the
needle that he used.

When morning came, the tricksters announced
that the suit of clothes was ready.

    While one trickster pretended to fasten a pair of pants on the emperor, the other asked the emperor to stand still.

    "I do not want to stick you with my needle," he warned as he pretended to sew one last button on the invisible cape.

    "You know," the emperor remarked nervously, "this fabric feels lighter than air."

    "Indeed. It is so light, it feels as if you have nothing on," replied one of the tricksters. "This, of course, is the beauty of our fine cloth."

Feeling much better, the emperor took one more look in the royal mirror. "It truly is my finest suit ever!" he said.

The emperor paid the two tricksters their last purse full of gold coins. Then he announced that it was time for the Royal Procession to begin.

Now that the tricksters had made their fortune, there was no reason for them to stay at the palace any longer. They packed up their gold. Then they made their way down the back roads of the kingdom, never to be seen again.

Soon the townsfolk began to gather for the Royal Procession. They had heard about the emperor's new clothes, and they pushed and shoved one another to get the very best view. Each one was eager to find out who among them was wise and who was not.

At last the trumpets sounded. As the emperor
marched through the streets, the townspeople were
shocked. Never before had they seen their emperor
clad only in his underwear. But each one wanted to
appear wise, so they began talking loudly to one
another about the emperor's clothes.

"Look at the beautiful pants he is wearing! Isn't that an enchanting cape? Did you ever see such a fine jacket?" they called.

The success of his new suit made the emperor feel very proud. He waved to the crowd and walked a bit more slowly, hoping to hear even more.

That is, until one little girl called out, "Look! The emperor has no clothes. He is walking through town without a shirt or a cape. He is not even wearing trousers!"

"The child is right," whispered a few in the crowd. Soon word spread, and the truth was out. The townsfolk began laughing and agreeing with the little girl.

"The emperor has no clothes!" they shouted. "The emperor has no clothes!"

The emperor knew at once that his subjects were telling the truth. Unfortunately for the emperor, he was ruled more by vanity and pride than common sense. So he insisted on marching in his underwear until his Royal Procession was finally done.

Then the emperor hurried toward the palace. He hoped his subjects would soon forget how foolish he had been.